BAD KITTY

Gets a

BATH

Nick Bruel

SCHOLASTIC INC.
New York Toronto London Auckland
Sydney Mexico City New Delhi Hong Kong

ISBN: 978-0-545-16213-5

Copyright © 2008 by Nick Bruel. All rights reserved. Published by Scholastic Inc., 557 Broadway, New York, NY 10012, by arrangement with Roaring Brook Press, a division of Holtzbrinck Publishing Holdings Limited Partnership. SCHOLASTIC and associated logos are trademarks and/or registered trademarks of Scholastic Inc.

12 11 10 9 8 7 6   10 11 12 13 14/0

Printed in the U.S.A.   40

First Scholastic printing, December 2009

Book design by Jennifer Browne

For Jules, Jenny, Kate, Halley, Julie,
and the rest of the Fabulous Feiffers.

• CONTENTS •

As you read this book, you'll notice
that there's an * following some of the words.

Those words will be defined in the Glossary*
at the back of this book.

• INTRODUCTION •

This is how Kitty likes to clean herself.

SHE LICKS
HERSELF.

She licks her leg.

She licks her tail.

She licks her back.

And to clean her face, she licks her front paw and rubs it all over where her tongue can't reach.

9

Sometimes, Kitty will do this for hours.

UNCLE MURRAY'S FUN FACTS

WHO, ME?

WHY DO CATS LICK THEMSELVES?

This is a close-up of Kitty's tongue. It is covered with hundreds of tiny fishhook-shaped barbs called "papillae.*" These barbs help her to comb her fur as she licks herself. Her tongue will also serve to collect any loose fur that she could swallow.

Papillae are partly composed of fibrous protein called keratin. Do you know what else is made of keratin? *Your fingernails!*

HOLY SALAMI! THAT GOOFY CAT'S GOT HUNDREDS OF TINY FINGERNAILS ON HER TONGUE!

Kitty has to be careful.
Sometimes, if she
licks her fur too much,
she can develop a
HAIR BALL.

Hair balls
form in Kitty's
stomach when
she swallows
too much fur.

Sometimes, the
only way to get
rid of that hair
ball is to cough
it up.

GNNNNn...

Coughing up
a hair ball isn't
always easy.

They can be
stubborn.

HACK

And sometimes
those hair balls
can be pretty
darn big.

WARNING!

You should NEVER clean yourself
the same way as Kitty!

DAILY NOOZ

KID SENT HOME FOR BAD BREATH — ALL OVER BODY

SCHOOL EVACUATED

"I forgot that I ate a garlic and egg pizza for lunch," said the boy, seen here in this picture walking home and wishing to remain anonymous.

"Well, I saw my cat cleaning herself with her tongue," said the child. "So I thought to myself, 'Gee, that looks like it could work on me, too!'"

Officials predict that the school will be re-opened in about a week once health officials have dealt with

"We tried soaking the child in a solution made of toothpaste and mouthwash," said Principal Sarah Bellum. "But it just helped a little. We can only hope that this incident served as a warning to

So, this is how Kitty *USUALLY* cleans herself.

Sometimes . . .

every now and then . . .

Kitty needs . . .

a real . . .

· CHAPTER ONE ·

PREPARING KITTY'S BATH

Do you remember the last time you tried to give Kitty a bath?

DAILY NOOZ

ENTIRE FAMILY FLEES FOR LIFE

The grisly story began when a local family, unprepared for giving their beloved cat a bath, was forced to evacuate their house after the kitty went on a screaming, biting, spitting, and scratching rampage.

Animal control experts were called in to subdue the cat but refused to enter the house.

Said one officer, "We see this sort of thing every time someone tries to give a cat a bath.

The terrified family was found hiding in this hickory tree four miles from their home. All pleas asking them to leave the tree were met with shouts of "Eek," "Yipes," and "This is worse than when we ran out of food for the kitty."

"Oh, the screams! I shall remember the screams from that house in my nightmares," said neighbor Mrs. Edna Kroninger. "It was worse than the day they ran out o food for the kitty. I almost move out of the neig

BE PREPARED.

The first lesson that all cat owners must learn is that . . .

CATS HATE BATHS

For your own safety, please repeat this to yourself four thousand eight hundred ninety-three times.

It's not that cats don't *like* baths. It's not that cats have a difficult relationship with baths. It's not that cats chose not to vote for baths in the last election. It's not that cats would rather choose vanilla over baths. It's not that cats neglect to send baths a card on their birthdays. It's not that cats pick baths last when choosing sides for a kick ball game. It's not that cats think about baths in the same way a fire hydrant thinks about dogs. It's not that cats look at baths in the same way that a vegetarian looks at ten pounds of raw liver. It's not that cats once bought baths an awesome present that cost an entire month's allowance, and then baths didn't even have the decency to say "thank you."

It's simply that . . .

CATS HATE BATHS!

Think about it this way . . .

Uncle Murray's Fun Facts

WHY DO CATS HATE BATHS?

Despite what most people say, cats don't hate water. Fish live in water, and cats LOVE fish. So most cats don't mind getting a little wet.

But cats do HATE baths. That's because cats only like to get wet when they're the ones in control, when they choose to get wet. If someone else has decided to make them wet, they HATE it.

And if a cat *has* to get wet, the water had better be warm.

A cat's fur is very good at keeping her warm, but not so good at keeping her dry. So if a cat gets wet in cold weather, that poor cat will have a hard time getting warm again. And that poor cat can catch a bad cold.

So, cats should always be bathed in warm (NOT HOT) water.

ME, I LIKE TO SHOWER IN THE MORNING WHILE I SING OLD SHOW TUNES LIKE "SOMEWHERE OVER THE RAINBOW" . . .!

Cats hate showers, too. And they rarely sing old show tunes.

Now that you understand that cats hate baths (you will be tested), you will find it much easier to prepare Kitty's bath BEFORE putting her in it.

The following are some of the items you will need for Kitty's bath:

ONE BATHTUB

PLENTY OF WARM WATER

CAT SHAMPOO

SOAP

HANDHELD SHOWERHEAD

WASHCLOTH

BRUSH

KITTY-SHAPED BATHROBE

WITH HOOD

DRY TOWELS

AND . . .

You should play it safe and make sure you have these items as well.

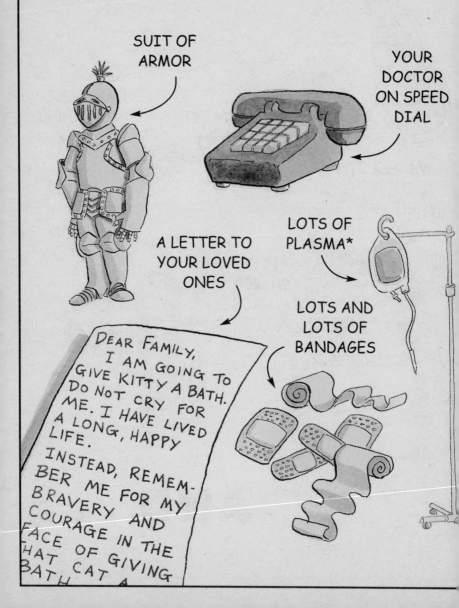

SUIT OF ARMOR

YOUR DOCTOR ON SPEED DIAL

A LETTER TO YOUR LOVED ONES

LOTS OF PLASMA*

LOTS AND LOTS OF BANDAGES

DEAR FAMILY,
I AM GOING TO GIVE KITTY A BATH. DO NOT CRY FOR ME. I HAVE LIVED A LONG, HAPPY LIFE.
INSTEAD, REMEMBER ME FOR MY BRAVERY AND COURAGE IN THE FACE OF GIVING THAT CAT A BATH

CLEAN UNDERWEAR
(BECAUSE STRESSFUL
SITUATIONS CAN CAUSE
"ACCIDENTS")

PLANE TICKETS
AND A MAP TO
YOUR AUNT
PAULINE'S HOUSE
WHERE YOU CAN
HIDE WHEN THIS
IS OVER

A SCRATCHING
POST MADE TO
LOOK LIKE YOU
THAT MIGHT
(BUT PROBABLY
WON'T) FOOL
KITTY

AN AMBULANCE IN
YOUR DRIVEWAY WITH
THE ENGINE RUNNING

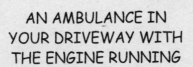

And, of course, the last thing you'll need before giving Kitty a bath will be Kitty herself.

But try not to say that out loud.

QUICK QUIZ

FILL IN THE BLANKS.

CATS _____

A) LOVE BATHS.

B) LIKE BATHS.

C) HATE BATHS.

D) ARE SMALL, FLIGHTLESS, DO-MESTIC FOWL EASILY RECOGNIZED BY THEIR COMBS AND WATTLES* THAT CAN LAY AS MANY AS 250 EGGS A YEAR.

ANSWER: The correct answer is C. If you answered anything other than C, please reread Chapter One 753 more times or until you are saying "Cats Hate Baths" out loud in your sleep. If you answered D, please go immediately to an eye doctor, because the animal in your home that you think is a cat is really a chicken.

• CHAPTER TWO •

FINDING
KITTY

Now's the hard part.

The bath is ready, but Kitty is not. In fact, Kitty is nowhere to be found.

Is she in her litter box?

Is she under the sofa?*

Is she sitting on her favorite window ledge?

NOPE.

Is she sitting in her favorite chair?

NOPE.

Is she lying in your bed?

NOPE.

So where is Kitty?

Kitty's very good at hiding. So maybe the best step right now would be to think about where you found her all the other times she hid.

This is where she was hiding when you had to take her to the vet.*

This is where she was hiding when you had to brush her teeth.

This is where she was hiding when you had to give her medicine.

This is where she was hiding when you had to clip her nails.

This is where she was hiding when you told her to finish her vegetables.*

There's Puppy!

Maybe Puppy knows where Kitty is hiding.

Hey, Puppy . . . Do you know where Kitty is hiding?

DUHHH... ARF?!

Hmmm . . . Maybe he doesn't know.

Hold on . . . Since when does Puppy have black fur? Puppy has never had black fur. So maybe that isn't Puppy at all. So who is it really? Hmmm . . .

IT'S KITTY IN DISGUISE!

GET HER!

SHE'S RUNNING UPSTAIRS!
GET HER!

SHE'S IN THE BATHROOM! She's trapped. Now, all we have to do is calmly close the door, and we can begin her bath.

Uh-oh.

• CHAPTER THREE •

HOW TO
GIVE KITTY
A BATH

Now that you have Kitty, and the bath is prepared, please follow these simple steps carefully so that both you and she are comfortable during the bath.

1) Gently but firmly gather Kitty up in your arms.

2) Pet her and caress her lovingly to reassure Kitty that all is well.

3) Tell Kitty that you love her. No doubt, Kitty will tell you that she loves you, too.

4) Now, gently lower Kitty into the warm, soapy water for her bath.

OH MY!
THIS ISN'T
SO BAD!

I AM QUEEN ESMERELDA,*
KITTY OF MAGIC CANDY
RAINBOW ISLAND!

I HAVE BEEN SENT TO
YOUR LAND TO FIND THE
ONE WITH THE TRUEST
AND BRAVEST HEART, FOR
ONLY THE ONE WITH THE
TRUEST AND BRAVEST
HEART WOULD DARE TO
GIVE A DIRTY, SMELLY
KITTY A BATH!

AS A REWARD FOR YOUR
TRUE AND BRAVE HEART,
I BESTOW UPON YOU
THE GREATEST TREASURE
EVER GRANTED . . .

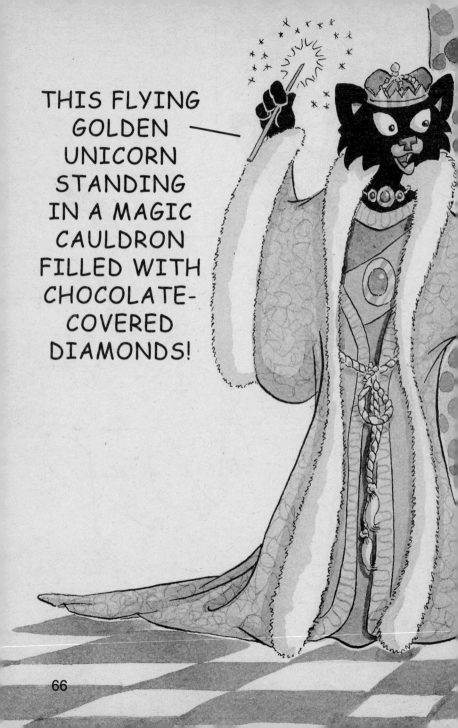

THIS FLYING GOLDEN — UNICORN STANDING IN A MAGIC CAULDRON FILLED WITH CHOCOLATE-COVERED DIAMONDS!

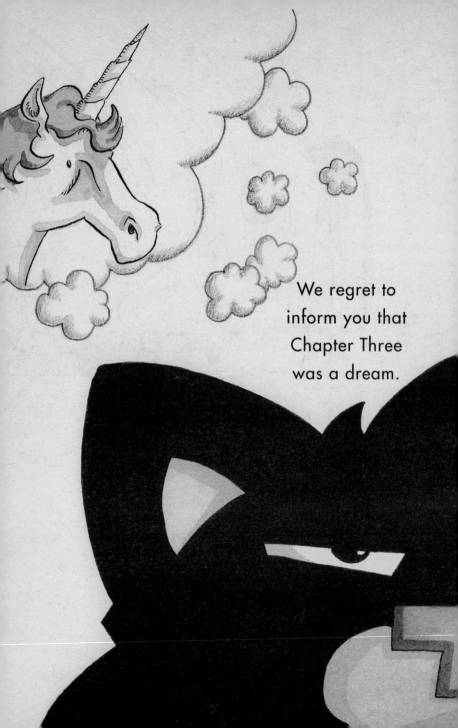

We regret to inform you that Chapter Three was a dream.

· CHAPTER FOUR ·

GETTING KITTY INTO THE WATER

You must have known it would be harder than that.

Now that you've regained consciousness, you probably remember what happened when . . .

You took her to the vet.

You made her
brush her
teeth.

You made her take her medicine.

You clipped her nails.

You made her finish her vegetables.

Nick,
I'm sorry, but this image is much too gruesome and violent for us to publish in this book. If we were to show what Kitty did here, we would give the readers nightmares for at least fifty years.

Your editor,*
Neal

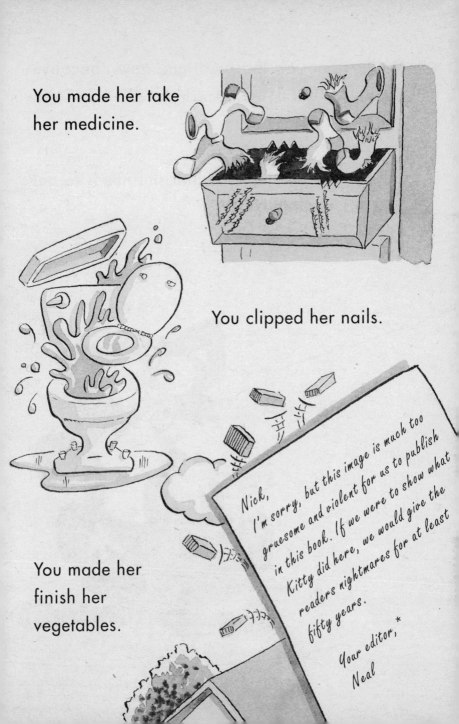

Well, none of that matters now, because Kitty . . . YOU STINK! And you NEED TO TAKE A BATH.

Tell Kitty in a firm voice that she needs to get into that bathtub NOW!

Okay. That didn't work.

You might want to try the subtle art of NEGOTIATION.*

Negotiation is how you can use words instead of force to try and convince Kitty to do something she doesn't want to do.

First, try FLATTERY.

LOOK AT THE PRETTY KITTY!
SUCH A SWEET, WONDERFUL,
PRETTY KITTY! DOESN'T THE
PRETTY, PRETTY KITTY WANT
TO BE ALL NICE AND CLEAN
AND SMELL JUST LIKE A
BEAUTIFUL FLOWER? WHAT
A PRETTY KITTY! WHO IS
THE PRETTIEST KITTY IN THE
WHOLE WIDE WORLD?
YOU ARE! YES, YOU ARE!
YOU PRETTY, PRETTY,
SWEET LITTLE KITTY, YOU!

If that doesn't work, try . . .

. . . BEGGING.

PLEASE! PLEEEEASE!
PLEASE GET IN THE BATHTUB!
PLEEEASE!
IF THERE IS EVEN AN OUNCE
OF GOODNESS IN YOU,
WON'T YOU PLEEEASE
GET IN THE BATHTUB?
PLEEEASE!
I'VE WORKED SO HARD TO GET
YOU HERE AND NOW YOU'RE
ALMOST IN THE TUB! YOU'RE
SO CLOSE! WON'T YOU
PLEEEASE GET IN THE TUB?
PLEEEEEEEEASE!

I'LL BE YOUR BEST FRIEND.

If that doesn't work, try . . .

. . . BRIBERY.

OH, KITTY . . . YOU KNOW THAT FANCY SCRATCHING POST MADE OUT OF SILK AND RHINOCEROS HIDE YOU LIKE? WELL, I'LL BUY IT FOR YOU IF YOU GET IN THE TUB. AND YOU LIKE THOSE GOAT TAIL AND SALMON FIN TREATS, DON'T YOU? I'LL BUY YOU THE BIGGEST BOX IN THE STORE IF YOU GET IN THE TUB. DID I SAY "BOX"? I MEANT "BARREL"! DID I SAY "BARREL"? I MEANT "TRUCKLOAD"! AND YOU CAN EAT THEM WHILE YOU TAKE YOUR BATH. DO WE HAVE A DEAL, KITTY?

KITTY?

If that doesn't work, try . . .

OKAY . . . IF YOU DON'T WANT
TO TAKE A BATH . . . FINE!
DON'T TAKE A BATH. SEE IF I
CARE. YOU'LL SMELL TERRIBLE
FOR THE REST OF YOUR LIFE
AND NO ONE WILL LIKE
BEING NEAR YOU, BUT THAT'S
OKAY BY ME. WHATEVER YOU
DO, DON'T GET INTO THAT
BATHTUB. THAT'S THE ONLY
WAY YOU'LL GET CLEAN, AND
WE WOULDN'T WANT THAT.
I'M HAPPY YOU'RE NOT GOING
TO TAKE A BATH. I REALLY
AM. I HOPE YOU NEVER, EVER
TAKE A BATH . . . UNLESS . . .

YOU REALLY WANT TO.

DO YOU?

Oh, well . . . It looks like Kitty is not going to be taking a bath after all. Sorry. We really tried, though.

Maybe we should just end the book right now and save some paper.

It really is too bad, because the only way we'll be able to give *Puppy* a bath is if Kitty goes first.

Didn't you know that, Kitty? Puppy is even dirt-ier and smellier than you. He's going to need an EXTRA SPECIAL BATH . . .

But, of course, that's never going to happen if Kitty doesn't take her bath first.

Well, I'll be . . .

· CHAPTER FIVE ·

THE
BATH

Now that you finally have Kitty in the bathtub, gently use a cup or small pot to pour warm bathwater over her to soak her fur.

Try not to pour water directly onto Kitty's head. Instead, use a soft, moist towel and gently wipe her face and head.

Use a cat shampoo recommended by Kitty's veterinarian to clean her dirty fur.

Rinse Kitty off using a handheld shower attachment if you have one. If not, gently pour water over her as you did earlier.

Again, try not to soak Kitty's head, and use that washcloth to wipe excess soap and water from her face.

Keep rinsing and soaking and wiping Kitty until you're absolutely certain you've removed all of the shampoo.

You may have noticed that Kitty's been making a lot of noise. She's probably trying to tell you something. The following is a list of common cat sounds and their meanings.

MEOW ⟶ I am hungry.

MEEE
OOO ⟶ I am very hungry.
WWW?

MEE   I'm pretty darn
OOW   hungry, and you
RRR ⟶   better feed me
OWW   right now or suffer
RRR!   the horrible
         consequences.

FFT! ──────→ I want to
be alone.

HISSS! ──→ Back off, pal!

MEOWR
REOWR ──→
FFT!

Unless you're
really tired of
living, please
respect that I
am in a very
bad mood.

MEOWR
REOWR
YEOWR
HISS
FFT ──→
FFT
FFT
MEOWR!

Nick,
Sorry, but once again we can't
print this. What Kitty says is
so horrible and repulsive that
we could all go to jail for the
rest of our lives if this was
printed.
Hope you understand.
Your editor,
Neal

You now have a very, very clean Kitty, even though she is also a very, very wet Kitty.

Gently remove her from the bathtub and drain the bathwater.

Dry Kitty off by wrapping her in a clean towel and rubbing her all over.

And Kitty will be nice and dry!

What a clean, sweet-smelling Kitty!

UNCLE MURRAY'S FUN FACTS

I'LL BE RIGHT BACK. I'M MAKING A SANDWICH!

CAN CATS SWIM?

Even though cats hate baths and aren't very big fans of water in general, ALL cats CAN swim. In fact, they're very good swimmers.

One breed of cat known as the Turkish Van loves to swim so much that they will jump in water whenever possible.

Tigers are also excellent swimmers. They live in very warm climates, so they tend to swim a lot to keep themselves cool.

If you're ever being chased by a tiger, don't bother jumping in the water. It won't help. Instead, climb a tree. Tigers love to swim, but they're not very good tree climbers.

And if you're ever around the wetlands of Nepal and Myanmar, look for the Fishing Cat. It's a breed of cat with long claws that never fully retract that dives into water to catch fish.

WHAT DID I MISS?

• CHAPTER SIX •

AFTER
THE
BATH

After the bath is done, Kitty will probably start licking herself quite a bit again. She'll want to be clean in the way she likes to be clean— cat-tongue clean.

This would *NOT* be a good time to pet her.

In fact, Kitty may avoid you altogether for a few
hours . . . or days . . . or weeks.

Try not to take it personally. After all, you made Kitty do something that she *HATED* and never wanted to do.

You still did the right thing. Kitty probably won't thank you now. She probably won't thank you EVER. She may even do little things in the next few days to tell you how angry she feels.

BRAND-NEW SNEAKER

SOMETHING AWFUL INSIDE

But if you had not given Kitty that bath, she would have licked herself while she was so very, very dirty. She could have become very, very sick. And neither you nor Kitty wants that!

COUGH

WHEEZE

BELCH

You and Kitty may not always get along. But there are TWO things you both have in common.

1) You both know that someday Kitty will forgive you.

2) You both hope you NEVER have to give Kitty a bath again.

· EPILOGUE ·

HOW TO GIVE PUPPY A BATH

HEH HEH HEH!

STEP ONE:

PUPPY

HOSE

· THE END ·

MEOWR
REOWR
YEOWR
HISS
FFT-FFT-FFT
MEOWR.

• GLOSSARY •

Bath • A word you should never say out loud around Kitty.

Combs and Wattles •
Fleshy lobes often found on the heads and necks of chickens but rarely found on cats.

COMB

WATTLE

NOT A CAT

Editor • Someone who *brilliantly* supervises the publication of a book like this one *and really deserves most of the credit.*

Esmerelda • The name of Nick Bruel's kitty at home.

Glossary • A list of words and their definitions often found at the back of a book. You have five seconds to find the Glossary for THIS book. Go!

Negotiation • A process that works very well when trying to convince your parents to give you a bigger allowance, but very poorly when trying to convince Kitty she needs a bath.

Papillae • The hundreds of tiny little hooks on Kitty's tongue that make it feel like sandpaper when she licks your finger.

Plasma • The liquid part of blood. Blood cells float around in it to carry fuel and oxygen around the body. Without plasma, they would be like fish trying to swim without a river. Having some extra plasma around when giving Kitty a bath is useful in case you "lose" a little.

Reverse Psychology • A method you can use to get someone to do something by pretending that you want the opposite. But it never works, so don't try it.

Sofa • A soft, comfortable, and very expensive scratching post used by Kitty.

Vegetables • Another word you should probably never say out loud around Kitty.

Vet • An abbreviation of *veterinarian*. A veterinarian is a doctor for animals like Kitty and may be the bravest person on the planet.

• ABOUT THE AUTHOR •

NICK BRUEL has written and illustrated some pretty funny books, including *Poor Puppy*, *Boing*, and *Who Is Melvin Bubble?* HOWEVER, he is currently wanted in 37 states as the creator of *Bad Kitty* (available in regular and special Cat-Nipped editions), about which some very important people said:

★ "Perhaps the hammiest, most expressive feline ever captured in watercolors." —*Kirkus Reviews* (starred review)

★ "Will have youngsters howling with laughter." —*Publishers Weekly* (starred review)